Oh, Fae-Folk

Cl

A collection of sho ..ngle verse poems

Independently published by Clive Culverhouse, UK.

Also by Clive Culverhouse available as ebooks on Amazon Kindle and paperback from Amazon.

The Opals of Ohbard and Pell

Ohbard and Pell meet up over lifetimes and dimensions for exchanges and conversations.

Thought provoking philosophical dialogue poems both profound and humorous with a classical feel.

A Smatherlump Of Nonsense Poetry

With wide appeal these funny poems will entertain over and over with satisfying whimsical absurdity.

Entertaining humorous verse for all the family and most pets.

Empireland

Funny epic fantasy adventure

Cedric of Golloth must escape his homeland or be dead by morning. Who knew the book "Empireland" Ced was writing would be so dangerous in the wrong hands. Now Ced was being hunted but he has a plan. And a quill...

The Legend Of Heliodor

Magical fantasy adventure

Imagine growing up with an ancient sacred legend and finding out you're in it!

Introduction

Fae, fay, fey, fairy, faerie.

In the magical and mysterious dark secret underworld of the fae-folk their presence can be felt in the nature around us, sometimes hidden in plain sight; as long as you know not just where to look, but how to look, their mystical world might just be closer than you think.

Presented in this entertaining book are short single verse poems in a pleasing mix of rhyme and free form poetry. Herein lies a wealth of fantasy inspired by English and British folklore, myths and mythology, legend and fairy tale about fantastical beings such as hobgoblins, goblins, boggarts, imps, wraiths, demons, mermaids and many other ley-creatures that frolic under sun, moon and the ghostly midnight church bells, and let's not forget witches who also feature in these often dark fantasy poems.

This is an other-worldly collection of curious and intriguingly written poetry that beautifully exploits language, words and word play befitting of they, the fae-folk.

Introduction cont..

A note on the inspiration, writing style and deliberate misspelling of words.

I have chosen to write these short poems in an "old", archaic way which I felt was more in line with the subject matter and complemented it nicely. I believe this so-called dated style of writing adds to the feel of the folklore upon which the poems are based or imagined. However, the poems themselves may not always necessarily tell of actual established folklore, there are many detailed books that cover folklore tales, but more a representation of the creatures within folklore and, on my part, with a poetic license. Also the poems are about how certain natural conditions such as weather or a flowery garden can make one feel a secret world is at work around us. The style of the writing here helps with that feel and compliments the poetry.

The inspiration for these poems has come in a variety of ways. Of course there are the folklore tales, myths and legends that feature otherworldly creatures, but also personal experience. By this I recall when I let my dogs out last thing at night and in the moonlit darkness I could hear the distant church bells chiming the hour eerily over the village. Or whilst once walking to work and seeing a solitary crow perched on a lone branch against the backdrop of a white winter sky. Or seeing dandelion seeds wisp along on the breeze. In all of these examples I could, under the right frame of mind, readily believe in a magical underworld.

I have written some of the poems in a way that might be easily remembered and recited like a saying or nursery rhyme. Imagine a family sitting having a picnic upon grass, seeing buttercups and then reciting a short four line verse suggesting the appeasement of goblins upon whose territory they may be encroaching and to let them pass before any trouble occurs. Or upon seeing the moon in the blue sky of day and reciting a poetic saying about its fictional meaning. Who knows, one day long after I have moved on to meadows afar, some of these verses may be quoted and told to future generations.

I have used the term "ley-creatures" often in my poems here, I may even have coined the term referring them to fae folk, although I shouldn't take credit for something I cannot prove.
The inspiration and idea of this is based on ley lines. Certain energies are believed by some to flow along these hypothetical conduits linking ancient structures and landmarks not just across the United Kingdom but the whole world. Therefore there would be an energised link, a pathway if you will, between Stone Henge in Wiltshire, England and the Pyramids in Egypt as an example. Ley lines have never been scientifically proven but their existence is believed by many and has become popular.
So my idea that the many fantastical, mystical entities and beings roaming the British Isles (and indeed many other countries) do so by following these theorised ley lines.
Fairies, goblins and perhaps even large exotic black cats, or the popular folkloric black dog - Black Shuck - phantom or otherwise may indeed use the network of ley lines roaming mysteriously from one part of the country to another as ley-creatures. These folklore and legendary beings like fairies, elves, trolls and goblins are hugely

important and prolific in popular culture so why shouldn't they have their own network of travel and escape? Afterall, pixies have known connections to stone circles, barrows and henges.

Upon the writing itself I have adopted an unorthodox approach in which words are often intentionally misspelled for the purpose of aiding pronunciation and to hopefully allow the reader to know how I intended the words to be read. This way of writing can be considered as experimental poetry as I have experimented on the words and their form and, of course, experimentalism is a known genre of poetry. The result of this utilisation of misspelled words, in most cases, is therefore resulting in adding an additional syllable to suit the line, its flow and its rhythm.

Many of these words, instead of ending "ed" now end "ied" or "id"; an example is the poem Queen of the waterfall:

Queen of the waterfall
wash thy whiten flowid hair
cascade curls foam rockid crop
down to the pools below

the words "flowid" and "rockid" force an extra syllable, opposed to "flowed" and "rocked" which do not. Another example is changing the two syllable word "worldly" into a three syllable word "worldedly".

Some other word endings have also been playfully used, i.e. ending a word with "ness" on words that do not usually have this ending, for example twelveness. Altogether these poems are a word play feast that I hope only enhances the poetry.

Please be assured this book of poetry is not full of typos, it is all meticulously worked and absolutely deliberate. Any odd or seemingly incorrect words are merely for the general feel of the poems or for how I wanted the reader to read them. CC

Oh, Fae-Folk,

Tell do tell of petal verse
whisper leaves into thine ear
for off on wind and breeze regale
from berry lips and fruited tongue
and wing of lace therein

What is this space I see between
yet not to thy fair maiden's eye
but mine own whose see is worldedly
and now, pray, worlds I see in worlds
a half-sight, unapparent, dream

Wind, whispered she
are the wings and feet of fae
brushing and frolicking the hour
and sad are they, fae
on the calm and still day

Devil's own thou tramplid hoof
ley-creatures bed 'pon ancient way
and to a call lost eon 'go
and standeth strong do rock
and standeth strong do they

Stirring a cauldron with a broom
left, a flake in a sweetened cone
one tooth witch this sweetening
tongue sweet her lashing spoon

What ley-creature visits my night
who shadows my every corner
do elven eyes upon me stalk
or goblin do you linger

Caw the crow's harsh rasp
quwaar the carrion carries
kaaarr cut through window's glass
ghaarr to a corvid's sharpened wake
mist yet not thy stifler's grasp

For thrice ye crow
on branchied arm
oh Morrighan tell
thy fate, thy harm

Due moon awaits thy tollied bell
among some roof and lowered lamp
awakied fae from tree and green
yet though the gravestone rested thee
come fore the churchied call

One, two, three buttercup
there are goblins on the grass
four, five, six buttercup
better let the goblins pass

Cobwebbed well 'gainst greying black
cornered dark by cold pane's breath
of dropletted catch Novemberedness
and ease not, does this my midnight
with her spells here dwell?

What is this house if not a tomb
for ageness hoods ago did scream
and scream upon a stair and saw
a grey, an absentee, am wraith
for in these roamings I narymore

Master sleeps with snorid wrath
but downstair creak floorboardedness
hobgoblin craft a busy hand
thou ear unto a distant bell
and churchied tolling's toil

For petal be thy colouried wing
see flutter gently as of lace
doth hide in free plain sight among
go fae as leaf caught 'pon thine air
and weave your magik near

Thistle be your crown thy fae
and 'pon a garden's rear you dwell
to rule and reign the petal queen
yet does not a manied nettle serve
as harbingers, yours and theirs

Panelled wall a passaged dwell
secret runningness hiders creep
but a boggart deepens a house
does he and rales within spacety
shall this lung its tubes to breath
an air of scurrilous dire mischief

A crow then two crows more did pass
and by the yew the breeze then blew
to spread the heads of seeds anew
and away the crow then two crows flew

Gravestones thy teeth of a churched mouth
gnaw of restless halfworlds recented away
and does a night of mid visit me walkers
to rap with skinnied knuckle on not
my door but my head, their moon call?
for aches it, my morning poundles reek

Afore the fae-folk undertake
a manied flower revival thy
gaze from window pane a'by
and secretly a'colour make
for say, they, spring be nigh

Crow crow watching you
tell the fairy folk to hide
crow crow watching you
. . . then tell them. . .
come out!
when you're inside

Wraith be your night a monotoned zest?
or I the colour you seek
in this of impeccable houred lust
pickings dealed of an unsaluted wanderer

Mermaid swim
thy golden sea
speak of Man
their prophecy

When gothic calls am I of listenied veil?
these shirks of arch and imp
dwellered somewhere within
for should this I leakied my telling
and foresaw scratchings in thy stone

A night dolk came to me as sleep played
put scratches on my back and reddened my eye
sewn aches to limb and planted irkings in my head
must now my day, I, of night dolk, suffer thee

Nature's lore bring forth thy tune
when garnished secrets pour the light
and knowing hand in watchful moon
where seeks insight from giving land
and laid from mind correspondences
preserved in magic's brine

Fae-folk brush thy flower heads
and runneth river of mead
through twilight's hollied glade
they pass . . .
and sway, they, oft' unseen

Witch your brew of witches past
air a charm of centuried zest
you burned with burners
you hung with hangers, now
be your bubbling pot glowing

Seen through the eye of a hag stone
underworlds enlist nay ensnare
but shaken not thy eye's hand
that reaches but in whom in me
grabs to do the seeing back

An imp will strile
n strawl at noon
but stray the hour
to steal the moon

What cries this breeze within a wind
encircle thy grand cathedral
an imp, oh imp whose cry in vain
of gargoyle now
stone, your partner's made

[Lincoln Cathedral]

Behold in sea and lake thy mer
enchanting song oh welcome voice
too through a shell against thine ear
a siren, her allure

Yet he did ought thy shadow of an underside
present be in low nightly light and lingered
stalkingied toward my skippied heart
in hope of some fearied death for will my
haunting demise quench his ashen thirst?

Waistcoated man oh wasted man
your trunk be only mottled shoes
lest your darknessed nights alone
be purged of a lover's moonlight

Daytime moon
out too soon
moon before night
see the fairies fight

This quillied pen kiss thy parchment
of stonied bottled ink and sight your
wordings of coil and curse, may too
a witches call foul a reader's cure
for thee, tis set, ye honeytrap

Blown dandelion head
your charms a'spread
be carried fae-folk on the flow
for drift thy imp and goblin go

Under-ones gather
make ready this fluted vessel of ichor
and ceremonied a worth to fill
make feast make merrimentied table
and downied this pallid mead
second realm, thee, and enter not?

Colded air gainst fog and treed
  sat rooked and waited high
for dawn had passed a momently
  but linger corvid's cry

and cry she screamed a deathedly
  to pierce the secreted hour
for only she could see through mist
  an underworld greyed dour

What, fog, do you hide when upon descends
for change that there whereon your toll
we, left, unknowing until picturesque thy fill
and whose sight blinded, was it not your own
to turn thine eye to a devil's bidding?

Low fielded mist thou carpeted entrance
rollied out from your otherworldly door
where there may treadied of creature
wise yet allowed does your cloak
bear a beguilied foot to cross upon?

Yet doth my qualm measure me
in hoping for a darkied sky
that I might argue exchange
with our many nightied demon
and comrades do he and I dawn

Though imp, goblin, demon be
this manied world and corneried
where from a shadow as of door
such halflies come and go

Oh boggart come
thy trickied sprite
play your tip-tap
feet this night

Roil this shadow over a groundied stage
but not a bodied cast be there
no dancied performer quells thine eye
yet a shadow, from whence this shadow
has not a day a silhouette?

What bringeths air to thy coolied neck
that hangied this morn, this noosied grasp
of hooded 'cutioner sent mine off to glade
and path, hath not the next air welcomed?

Fae and mer on land and lake
a sharied strain of common past
related now by a mistied haze
and beckon do thy reckoning
appease thine ancient wrath

Cookied in a couldroned pot
stir thy thought of cursedies
lake loss shine and ripplied gloss
to a deathelesied rot

A night within a night
does not the eve's camber suggest
and echoed dull thy churchied toll
to call upon those underlies by
who treadied roof and ears

Strike ye of a midnightied bell twelven calls to thee
through latied haze from streets away oft' her song
a rallied call to arms amid a moon whose pallid eye
from wisp of drifting cloud assigns the night and all
a night can jeer go beckonied from the demon bell
and rise go play an underworld ye make a belly full

Once jar the castle 'pon scapied scene
now sterling 'lith heroic of thy land
yet in a wall of wallied stone do not
mere ghostied phantoms stalk in spear
defending from green's underlees

On this sweet season do you
braid thy heartstrings in
loomied blanket, be calm
within these wrappied arms
and slake an autumn's crave
but restless be a foresteer
of darkened tree and risen
thy demon undergrowth
to weave their wickedness

On a solitary moment to midnight
wraiths be readying fair sleeper
and does not your half-wakied turn
in sweat betray thy wraithen brawl
and 'pon dawn awaken scratched

Devil mint thy master's coin
that may be spentied in thou reach
o' mortal soul whose heart beseech
for 'pon death repayment, join

Goblin spare your heresies this eve
and walk among the sunnied folk
oh half lit stage thou normalcy
but breach thy boundaried haul

There's a twelveness to the two
a.m. of a nightied trapped of moment
and of creatures caught in hiding ear
go lightly sway the velvet drapes
for the shapes of those surround

And from what spell sake thee
among steamied haze by chance
widdershin moon releasied
yet know thy place
nettle sly 'twixt flower
for thou shalt not tooth
thy summoning hand

A'breathe a hob folkloried in a shire's depth
and he, his kith 'n kin beneath their shadow
roam doth roam thy roses lot
around late night fires he watcheth on
thou spake the tongue of time

Be not the dawn that shaketh me
be not the dew of morning earl
be not the stag's presided mist
but of charge in gloss's greenery
be hob and sprite expectantly

Trail he did layeth down
acorn cup and feathered fern
for though its canopy shelters thee
and halls a treelayen corridor
as guide, the green man chaperone

Places of a place's shadow
where movied, once doth dwell
yet loudness be an emptied space
oh brownie and your handling hands
yay you, nay not my fraying mind

Hide ye among the daisy heads
yellow face, white petalled hair
and fae you warming free and fair
then sleepeth in the flower beds

Bow the fae
on bended wing
as goblin may
on gnarlied knee

Rest upon my grave, he said
and wait for me at midnight's toll
at first chime shall we dance and play
at second be thy devilment
then on 'til our eleventh bell
on twelfth he dived back underground
then. . . rest upon my grave, he said

Under a henge hides he and she
near an ecurie for equine frivolity
to neatly plait a golden mane
then ride and play in pixie's name
at night near mid of star and moon
to slake the pangs of puckish tune
and well they may have built the henge
in ancient time and dwelled there since

See a lane not stone or road
but trackway path of fae-folk steps
and of thy hedgied line must be
of light and nimble lest thou bruise
the solitude of their resting daze

Worlds within worlds go spinningied
as master sits at marbled desk
ponders and looks upon each turn
for some it's here or onto fae
and life the door that welcometh
yet death be not thy final knock

Water's way o'er water's grave
thy ripplid foam and bubbled scream
for loch see kelpie taketh she
'pon dawn another down

Beware the hidden dip my friend
where redcap kneels a' drinkingid
the crimsoned blood thy lifeliness
but all now spill and stain amade
be wearied oh this trail

Goblin's Posy
a bouquet of thistles
and a vased cut of nettles
thorned stems devoid of leaf
bountiful head and petals

Dew drop seep down bank and brae
thy bracing nip for elven lip
and though a tongue of ancientced
doth quench thy duskid voice

Do not sadden on this morrowed morn
though she the nymph will soon upend
for long hath fern and berry wheeled
and all a'gather, wake unto yet
does thy leaf not wipe tree tears?

Sugar is as sugar is
and sweet as petal's aroma
for just as breath adjoins thine air
then worlds a'blend
then worlds a'partner
hold, thy sugar tooth

Fae thy ride on the midnight back of a raven
wings weave the devils torch
for he sees not thy feather and lace
take flight and leave thou countered ways
see torchlight grimace, diminished

Under a henge hides he and she
near an ecurie for equine frivolity
to neatly plait a golden mane
then ride and play in pixie's name
at night near mid of star and moon
to slake the pangs of puckish tune
and well they may have built the henge
in ancient time and dwelled there since

Goblin tears hath not a rainid morn
sullen in thy mimicry though see
a window be a mirror?
relinquish thy cloud for sun
oh goblin for he departs

Kwaar thy rook be thy tempest roar
of thunder yet blackened as he to sky
and glint does his eye oh fleetingid
be not thy lightning's angry curse?

What hand reachid out
from bridge's 'neath
came grab
came drag
came sharpid teeth

Pale green lacewing
be not you fae
still then dancing
when ne'er I see

White stallion rear on hinds
as pixie 'ward horizon slopes
and flow silver mane, flowid on
'til pixie 'turns this dawn

Hide 'mong hedgerow thy sprites
be you oh blushing face
of hawthorn berries this sun
and hark your whisperid songs
as twilight's breeze uncovers thee

Oh colourless be thy crow
who taunts 'pon silhouetted tree
dawnid mist thy blendid winter
yet be your presence
does not a vibrant black revere?

Gather ye thou restive mer
a tale flick too far
and sleepeth under moonid eve
then wake anew
then swim adieu
and gone the mer-folk are

Mine own devil come walk with me
and tread as I on greenied ground
yet see among me buttercups
thou tameth, be thy calm

Green leaf be that your hat
for riches of bud and petal fist
oh leprechaun ye guard thy wealth
then treasures bloom
your rainbow of vibrantness

Green man send your fae to work
be your ley-creatures under leaf
among thy forest, garden, copse
for goodly deed or do mischief

Who lives beyond the waterfall
why the white-gowned elven queen
beyond the mists a'throned she sits
for in silver droplets, reign

Battlegrounded hill and moor
for boulders lie a'strewnid there
rock war seal thine ogre's wrath
yet giant bodies still remain
thy corpse among the grass

Jackdaw thieve thy maker's gold
then sit upon a thatchid roof
await doth gatherid thee folk
for a newborn cry replacid wealth

gnome protect the garden bloom
gnot be teasing as you do
gnow above the ground may you
gneatly tend the greens that grew

Pack horse bridge oh crumblid stone
of age remain within the new
yet not does troll a'settle still?
to they who cross, spring forth ahoy
best choose thy payment carefully

What secret told the sycamore
to elm, to oak, that autumn day
when leaf 'pon leaf a'droppid down
and all a'shed their summer clothes
what secret told the sycamore
that settled all a'calm

To an overhanging hollow
where sleep fae folk under willow
and there adrift float seeds
like silver stars upon the breeze

A forest rears in hoofen plight
their trampling is nearing
the unicorns are restless
a pounding wind around us
'til calmid by a fae born king

Tree 'tween tree
to where the woodwose be
see, thee, see
beware the wild man, he

Bramble snakes along a winding beck
gentle feet a'splash a cloud
of silt like ash
but stay thy feet in water, wade
for thorns be not thy prison's guard?

You honed your way in sorcery, son
relinquished all, the hard of day
to see a softly land unfold
a wizard now, a wizard's way

Fae be spent upon a day
and sleep among the amethyst
renew anew she waiteth dawn
and of this rising sun go you

Buttercups where feast do fae
thy crumb a'shown as daisy heads
and 'pon a lawn a banquet had
near gone, though secret trace

Shift thy shape ye goblin cur
be head 'pon prickly thistle stem
then rogue ye 'mong the mourning stones
and watch the weepers weep

You look like you've seen a goat
the farm stayed between the hills
this valley staunch but animal ghosts
grazed on footpathers hiking through
their embittered pastures and well
if no stick poked upon deadstock

On the roof, on the roof
starling song
calling to the fairies "come along"
off the roof, off the roof
starling flies
stay away fairies until sunrise

Beseech a trepid finger through
foxed page of a grimoired host
and see of herb, of plant for do
embers of these spells pen their
inkied curse upon such wallow?

No stars no stars
overhead
all the ghosts
all the ghouls
are out of bed!

Pass under the lychgate
at the sixth stroke midnight bell
and affair with fae world creatures
the halflies, until stroke twelve

Wishing well oh wishing well
toss thy coin in the wishing well
though if caught by the troll
your wish be void but
on the well's ground be plentiful

Mood be changeth 'pon a whim
the eyes of nature screwid so
come frown come smile volatile
a tempered gust before a storm
be not thy devil's wrath?

Invisible for a mostly part
then what? a flying by?
catch thine eye
unveil thy faerie heart

Yellow calls from a cowslip
out from a tubular trumpet
a calling of goblins who will
appear from under a toadstool

Witch thy finger bonefully points
to a cat or a dog or wanderer thee
and change them into grotesquied light
of a wraith or a demon of cursid soul
to bid her wares throughout

Queen of the waterfall
wash thy whiten flowid hair
cascade curls foam rockid crop
down to the pools below

Oh spirit of thine ancient 'bode
of bull oak 'pon this wispid grove
and whom thy call be elf or ought
dwelleth in this hollow tree home

Goodness kept upon this step
and house beyond by wooden hare
bring calm to all and thee protect
and safe be they who liveth there

It spake of this upon a card
a change, a turn, a seeing new
what lies betwixt each blade of grass
what tilts the head of daisies so
the tarot spake its whir

It happened on a moonid eve
a banshee scream a'cut thine air
a'way a'way a'voicid cry
why colours are a'gone of night
and 'pon a house a death be there

Dance oh dance thy maypole stands
from earth to sky and ribbon strands
oh tree of life a'weave with thee
and bless Beltane's fertility

The giant's door to worlds within
a circle of thy standing stones
and pass into a such of time
just so just so just rightedly
move on to one more realm

A hole a hole within a tree
but not the tree the canopy
an eye an eye a'peaking out
the woodland face . . .
. . . and seeing owt

Fairy rings upon the grass
where oft' the fairies spritely dance
pick a daisy
pick a stone
away the fairies have thee gone

Curlid up and covered up
from the bogeyman a'neath my bed
and woe was there on creakid stairs
a nightid terror now a'dawn
oh dew be not thy bedtime tears?

Black Shuck thou stalketh such
glimpse thy head of sharpid fang
a grim of he an omen's hand
woe betide I to cross your path

Red hat thy dotted back
hide thee 'mong the ladybirds
red hat thy dotted back
with thee fae fly away

Murderous scream thy distant fox
across a fog and chimied bell
when night takes on a curtain fall
a call to gather ley-creatures
spread for thy widened scene

Witches three on a pig's back sat
and rode and rode under clothen hat
carried by swine down an earthen track
witches three on a pig's back sat

Lamppost light a hooded street
and catch sight of a shadow fleet
be quick it round thy cornerid
left trace an echoed eye

Who is this skin the Devil holds
lipped kiss of a moon's face
betrayer to a night's amour
loaned not sold, souled as she
the Devil's hold devoted

Leave your bedroom door ajar at night
do you? for thy inviting in
and sleep when takes a'creep do they
    pull your hair!
    thicken your tongue!
and morning sees you crumpled

With witch and their wily craft
of witchcraft
witchlike and witchy
from witching and witchery
by witches, witchlings and witchlets
which witch withal
   to be
witched, bewitched and crafted

She was a creature
half goblin, half goblin
in an ever widening
underworld
and all the other halflings
would creature their own
and world it a little wider

The heave and the hove of a half beast ahead
in the thread of a road and its kill of the dead
as it pulled with a pulling to a new place instead
for the leisurely lounging upon being fed

Redcap
come old Red
come lift your head
feast upon this fruit instead
yet you dine on blood of dead
soak your cap on all a'fed
come lift your head
oh come old Red

Enchanted forest listenid
to eery woolly whispering
and does thine ear beseech of thee
to heed thy pine and leaf

Rarely nay ever does one see
a creature dead and their body
when last a squirrel corpse be saw
let alone an elf or more
no, seeing tiny death a'where
oh where oh where 'tis very rare

Song for a king played she
the witch with a jews harp she
danced to bring the devil she
plucked thy witchcraft melody

Dear bent and twisted woodland tree
be you the sorcerer of your world
around you gather dark world folk
while shun be thy by other trees
yet you all wanderers see

Cave thy rock side mouth oh
fae folk lounge their home too
but oh fae folk what do you do
when without warning enters few
aye hide as stalagmites do you

Hark thy wind across the branch
play through woodland pipes be thee
oh forest music tend thine ear
when fauns abound by tree

What fae be this thy mandrake
in ritual cast be stirred and stoked
for does this form of figure become
the flight of broom, witch gathering

Solstice throw thy light and dark
upon the life and death of her
our mother nature spirals thus
and rebirth gives a newly verse
of cycle and thy term

Waves a'form foam on the wind
but underneath the water ways
be currents of thy coastal sea
the flowing hair of mermaids

Dare thy feet 'pon carpeted moss
walk softid 'neath thy canopy
for onto darkness as of cloud
be not thy heavy rustling
like thunder sung from thee?

Wings oh flutter be thy wings
be of feather, silk, and lace
they of feather oh thy bird
they of silk oh butterfly
but they of lace oh magic fae

Of those b'kneeled aside their pew
for above are gargoyle eyes on you
  waiting . . . then . . .
dismount a wall and dance about
when the church is emptied out

Air thy touch upon my skin
a gentle blow from nowhere but
does fly a graceful arc does she
for here a sylph a'passeth be

Spring on hill a drinking place
be where a gathering comes to
and while away an afternoon
do hidden ones in all a'grace

October be thy foremost month
of majesty and Halloween
but blossomed are the others too
with bud and bloom of lore

See two doves
  sat in a tree
wed ye will
  and lovers be

Who darkens a midday sky
by whom thy wrath be summoned
to turn thy leaf with angered wind
or bend thy stem of a flower's reach
and bellow rains upon

Given time on all a gravestone bends
and leans a'staggered obliquely
do hob and goblin rest upon
and push them crookedly

Church ground raised
its yard walls bowed
be bones within
all bursting out
and roam do they
on path and road

Pray tell what to do when a tree looks at you
with those sullen sunken knotty eyes
and then as he flashes those spindly twig lashes
and sappy tears when it comes to goodbyes

Save the trinket keep 'n' safe
shay o' jewel and steen
lest a boggart on his way
steals upon what's seen

[shay - admirable, steen - stone]

Do you hear the thunder
of ogres in the distance
getting ever closer as their
shuffling is persistent

Dear fae your violet be
with leafy wings of blueid tinge
and fly does she above all green
for sprinkle thy magic spread

They who see but nay do see
some wondrous shade amid the shoots
in all a vibrancy of a petal's song
oh pity they who see but nay do see
for fae be not thy shunner's world

Oh, fae-folk bless thy kin to thee
with tale and lore both grim and fair
then show themselves when thinnest be
the veil between our world and theirs

If you enjoyed reading my poems, please would you leave a review or just a few words, it doesn't have to be much, but your words would make it easier for others to find my book and help them to choose to read it.

Thank you
Clive Culverhouse

Printed in Dunstable, United Kingdom

70274661R00037